D1055516

The Boxcar Children Mysteries

THE BOXCAR CHILDREN
SURPRISE ISLAND
THE YELLOW HOUSE MYSTERY
MYSTERY RANCH
MIKE'S MYSTERY
BLUE BAY MYSTERY
THE WOODSHED MYSTERY
THE LIGHTHOUSE MYSTERY
MOUNTAIN TOP MYSTERY
SCHOOLHOUSE MYSTERY
CABOOSE MYSTERY
HOUSEBOAT MYSTERY
SNOWBOUND MYSTERY
TREE HOUSE MYSTERY
BICYCLE MYSTERY
MYSTERY IN THE SAND
MYSTERY BEHIND THE WALL
BUS STATION MYSTERY
BENNY UNCOVERS A MYSTERY
THE HAUNTED CABIN MYSTERY
THE DESERTED LIBRARY MYSTERY
THE ANIMAL SHELTER MYSTERY
THE OLD MOTEL MYSTERY
THE MYSTERY OF THE HIDDEN PAINTING
THE AMUSEMENT PARK MYSTERY
THE MYSTERY OF THE MIXED-UP ZOO
THE CAMP-OUT MYSTERY
THE MYSTERY GIRL
THE MYSTERY CRUISE
THE DISAPPEARING FRIEND MYSTERY
THE MYSTERY OF THE SINGING GHOST
MYSTERY IN THE SNOW
THE PIZZA MYSTERY
THE MYSTERY HORSE
THE MYSTERY AT THE DOG SHOW
THE CASTLE MYSTERY
THE MYSTERY OF THE LOST VILLAGE
THE MYSTERY ON THE ICE
THE MYSTERY OF THE PURPLE POOL
THE GHOST SHIP MYSTERY
THE MYSTERY IN WASHINGTON, DC
THE CANOE TRIP MYSTERY
THE MYSTERY OF THE HIDDEN BEACH
THE MYSTERY OF THE MISSING CAT
THE MYSTERY AT SNOWFLAKE INN
THE MYSTERY ON STAGE
THE DINOSAUR MYSTERY
THE MYSTERY OF THE STOLEN MUSIC
THE MYSTERY AT THE BALL PARK
THE CHOCOLATE SUNDAE MYSTERY
THE MYSTERY OF THE HOT AIR BALLOON
THE MYSTERY BOOKSTORE
THE PILGRIM VILLAGE MYSTERY
THE MYSTERY OF THE STOLEN BOXCAR
THE MYSTERY IN THE CAVE
THE MYSTERY ON THE TRAIN
THE MYSTERY AT THE FAIR

The Mystery of the Lost Mine
The Guide Dog Mystery
The Hurricane Mystery
The Pet Shop Mystery
The Mystery of the Secret Message
The Firehouse Mystery
The Mystery in San Francisco
The Niagara Falls Mystery
The Mystery at the Alamo
The Outer Space Mystery
The Soccer Mystery
The Mystery in the Old Attic
The Growling Bear Mystery
The Mystery of the Lake Monster
The Mystery at Peacock Hall
The Windy City Mystery
The Black Pearl Mystery
The Cereal Box Mystery
The Panther Mystery
The Mystery of the Queen's Jewels
The Stolen Sword Mystery
The Basketball Mystery
The Movie Star Mystery
The Mystery of the Pirate's Map
The Ghost Town Mystery
The Mystery of the Black Raven
The Mystery in the Mall
The Mystery in New York
The Gymnastics Mystery
The Poison Frog Mystery
The Mystery of the Empty Safe
The Home Run Mystery
The Great Bicycle Race Mystery
The Mystery of the Wild Ponies
The Mystery in the Computer Game
The Mystery at the Crooked House
The Hockey Mystery
The Mystery of the Midnight Dog
The Mystery of the Screech Owl
The Summer Camp Mystery
The Copycat Mystery
The Haunted Clock Tower Mystery
The Mystery of the Tiger's Eye
The Disappearing Staircase Mystery
The Mystery on Blizzard Mountain
The Mystery of the Spider's Clue
The Candy Factory Mystery
The Mystery of the Mummy's Curse
The Mystery of the Star Ruby
The Stuffed Bear Mystery

THE STUFFED BEAR MYSTERY

created by
GERTRUDE CHANDLER WARNER

Illustrated by Hodges Soileau

ALBERT WHITMAN & Company
Morton Grove, Illinois

ISBN 0-8075-5513-4

3 5 7 9 10 8 6 4 2

Printed in the U.S.A.

Contents

CHAPTER 1

An Unbearable Emergency

A roomy car carrying four children and their grandfather made its way up into the mountains. As the car climbed higher and higher, the children in the car yawned and stretched.

Six-year-old Benny Alden yawned twice to pop his ears. The car was so high up! The mountains must have grown while he'd been dozing. Now he was wide awake again. "Hey," he said. "What are those cotton balls on the hills?"

The other Alden children — Henry,

Jessie, and Violet—laughed along with their grandfather, James Alden.

Jessie, who was twelve, turned around from the front seat. "You'd better rub the sleep from your eyes, Benny. Those are sheep, not cotton balls. They still have on their thick winter coats. That's why they look so fat and fuzzy."

"Not for long," fourteen-year-old Henry said, ruffling Benny's brown hair. "Peggy and Doc Firman told Grandfather our visit is just in time to help them with sheep shearing. I'd like to see that."

"Know what I'd like?" ten-year-old Violet asked. "I'd like to help Peggy sew some of her Peggy Bears. Didn't she say we might get to do that, Grandfather? I hope so."

"I know so." Grandfather smiled at Violet in the rearview mirror. "When I told Peggy Firman how handy you are with a needle and thread, she couldn't wait for us to stay at Woolly Farm. She's got her hands full designing and sewing her teddy bears to sell at the Old Mills Teddy Bear Jamboree."

Benny reached into his backpack. He

pulled out a scruffy, sad-looking teddy bear that often went along on family trips. "I hope you don't get jealous of Peggy's new-looking bears, Mister B.," he told the stuffed brown bear.

"Mister B. is certainly showing his age," Grandfather Alden said. "He's traveled on quite a few trips since I was a boy."

Violet reached over to stroke the bear's droopy head. "Poor Mister B. I think it's time to bring you to Doctor Firman's Toy Hospital. You need some nice wool stuffing and a new eye."

Mister B. stared back at Violet with his one glass eye. Yes, it was time for a visit to the doctor's.

Mr. Alden slowed down when he reached Old Mills. "Awful lot of cars today," he said. "People are already arriving for the Teddy Bear Jamboree." Mr. Alden pointed to a small wooden building next to the Old Mills General Store. "There's Doc Firman's Toy Hospital."

"I wish we could go in right now," Violet said, disappointed to see a CLOSED sign.

"I guess someone else wants to go in, too. Look, there's a woman knocking at the window as if she sees somebody inside."

"Whoa!" Henry said as their car pulled up next to a yellow van. "Check out the big red bear. It's sitting in the front seat like a real person, with a seat belt on and everything."

Jessie giggled. "Who could it belong to? It looks funny sitting there — as if it's waiting for its owner to come back."

"Here comes that woman who was tapping on the window," Henry said. "The big bear must belong to her."

As soon as the woman got behind the wheel, she blew her horn for Mr. Alden to move.

Jessie rolled down the window. "Sorry. We're stuck in traffic, too. I like your bear."

"I have an emergency!" The woman honked again.

At last the traffic cleared up, and Mr. Alden pulled away. A few moments later, the woman passed the Aldens' car just outside of Old Mills. "Goodness, I wonder what kind of emergency she has," Mr. Alden said.

"A big red bear emergency," Henry said.

"Look, there's a sign for Woolly Farm!" Benny cried when the car rounded a curve in the road. "Half a mile."

Half a mile later, Grandfather drove up a long dirt road. By now the Aldens could see that the cotton balls on the hills had sooty black faces. The children rolled down their windows.

"Hey, sheep!" Benny yelled out. "Baa!"

"Baa! Baa! Baa!" the sheep bleated back.

At the end of the road stood a red house with a white porch all around. A few sheep munching on the front lawn looked up when the Aldens pulled in. Then they went right back to snacking on the grass.

A cheery woman with curly silver hair came out carrying a fluffy white-haired lamb. "Hello, Aldens!" the woman said when she saw the family. "I'm Peggy." She handed the lamb to Benny so she could give Mr. Alden a hug. "I'm so glad you brought

the children to stay with us," she said to Grandfather.

A smiling bearded man in farmer's overalls greeted the Aldens. "Welcome to Woolly Farm. I'm Raymond Firman, but everybody calls me Doc. I take care of live animals like that lamb you're holding and stuffed animals like this fellow." He nodded at Mister B., who was sticking out of Benny's backpack. "Mind if I take a look at him?"

Benny could hardly take his eyes off the lamb in his arms. "Sure, go ahead. His name is Mister B. Hey, you," he crooned to the warm fuzzy creature with the long black eyelashes.

"Baa!" the lamb cried back.

Grandfather looked around at all the animals scurrying about. "You seem to have more animals than people here."

Nearby, a yellow cat chased a squawky, but very quick, rooster.

"Don't worry about Rudy, our rooster," Peggy said. "Buttercup is too slow to catch him."

Two friendly dogs came around to sniff the Aldens one by one.

"The collie is Taf," Peggy told the Aldens. "The black mutt is Midnight," Peggy said. "We found him wandering around Woolly Farm one day, and he never left."

"That's how we got our dog, Watch," Violet told Peggy. "He wandered in from the woods to the boxcar we lived in after our parents died. Before Grandfather found us, Watch found us."

"And I'm certainly glad he did," Grandfather said. "Well, I'll take the suitcases from the car, children. After that, I'll be heading north for a couple days on business. So I'll say good-bye now."

The children each gave Grandfather a good-bye hug.

"Are we the only guests at Woolly Farm?" Jessie asked after Grandfather left.

"Oh, we'll have a full house by the time the Teddy Bear Jamboree opens," Peggy answered.

"Don't forget you-know-who," Doc whispered when a woman rushed toward everyone. "Hello, Miss Sayer. Meet the Aldens. They've come for the Teddy Bear Jamboree as well."

"Hi," Jessie said when she recognized the woman. "We saw you and your bear when we were stuck in traffic just a little while ago."

The woman, whose red and white polka-dotted hat seemed about to blow away, paid no mind to the Aldens. "I've been searching for you all morning, Doctor Firman. You keep disappearing on me. Well, never mind. I need you to check Chatter Bear right away."

The Aldens saw Peggy and Doc exchange looks as if this had happened before.

"Now, now, Miss Sayer," Peggy said. "I'm sure you'll want Doc to check Chatter Bear at the toy hospital so he can be examined properly."

The woman clamped down her hat, squashing the bow on top. "Well, I suppose so. But I will expect Chatter Bear to be your first patient when you open the hospital in the morning." With that, Miss Sayer stomped off in her green mud boots, carrying her orange plastic tote bag.

Doc smiled. "Miss Sayer is one of my regulars. She comes to the jamboree every year with some new bear she's designed or copied from old bears. She can't quite make a go of her bear business, though. Now she's hoping to interest a toy factory in making a talking bear."

Peggy sighed. "Every time we turn around, there's Miss Sayer and Chatter Bear. Yesterday I found her in my studio looking at fabrics. I think her bear has more outfits than I do."

Doc examined the Aldens' bear. He didn't have any kind of outfit at all. "Mister B. here is quite a different fellow than Chatter Bear. We'll have him on the mend soon. Bring him by in the morning, children. I have a soft spot for soft old bears like Mister B."

Standing on the hill, Peggy and the Aldens watched Miss Sayer struggle to get Chatter Bear out of her van.

"They're quite a pair," Peggy said. "I'm not sure Chatter Bear is quite ready for the jamboree. He has a few problems, what with his voice box and battery-powered eyes. Doc tried to tell Miss Sayer she might do better by designing a simple bear, but she won't listen."

Violet hugged Mister B. "I'm glad our bear doesn't have eyes that need batteries. He's only got one eye, anyway."

Peggy gave the Aldens' bear a gentle pat. "Never you mind, Mister B. I'm sure Doc will get you a new glass eye. We'll soon have plenty of natural sheep wool to fatten you up. Now let's go to Shepherd's Cottage. That's where you children will be staying. Don't mind the animal parade," she said when her pets followed everyone.

After the children got their suitcases, Peggy brought them by the barn. "This is where we shear our sheep and prepare the wool we use for my bears."

Peggy noticed Miss Sayer's yellow van parked next to the barn. "Oh, dear. I asked Miss Sayer not to go in there without one of us. She crashes around so, scaring the sheep. Besides, I really can't have her alone with all my wool-making equipment."

Benny tugged on Peggy's sleeve. "Can we go in there? I promise not to scare the lambs, especially this guy."

Peggy saw how gently Benny held the lamb in his arms. "Of course. Not right now, though." She stuck her head in the door. "Yoo-hoo, Miss Sayer. I'm locking up now."

Peggy clicked the padlock. "She must be somewhere else. I wish she would park in the area for the guests."

Soon they came to a small red and white cottage.

"Oh," Violet said when Peggy let the children inside Shepherd's Cottage. "It's like my room at home, with flowered wallpaper."

"Aw!" Benny said. "It doesn't look like where a shepherd would live. Couldn't we sleep in the hayloft like real shepherds?"

Peggy chuckled. "Taf and Midnight are our shepherds. If there's time, you're welcome to play in the hayloft. Just be careful climbing up. We keep the ladder outside so we can load the hay directly from the wagon. But it wouldn't be safe to sleep up there — you might roll off!"

"Here are some real beds." Violet put Mister B. down on one of them. His head flopped onto his chest.

"After you drop off Mister B. at the toy hospital tomorrow, I hope you can help us with the sheep shearing," Peggy said. "How does that sound?"

"Like fun!" Henry said. "Work is the best fun of all."

Peggy stepped onto the porch. "See you in the morning," she said.

Benny looked down at the lamb. "Hey, what do I do with this little guy? I don't want to wake him up."

Peggy pointed to a small wooden crate just inside the doorway. It was filled with clouds of fleece. "Just lay him down there. He can spend the night in here. If he wakes up crying, give him this." Peggy pulled a baby bottle from her jacket pocket. "Just make sure to keep him inside. It's still cold at night, and he needs to stay warm. And one other thing."

"What?" Benny asked.

"He needs a name," Peggy answered. "Your grandfather said you were good at naming things."

Benny stroked the lamb's black forehead for a minute. "Smudge. I'd like to call him Smudge."

CHAPTER 2

Baa, Baa, Bad Day

"Smudge was better than an alarm clock," Benny said the next morning when the children walked into Old Mills. "He woke me up a bunch of times, so I gave him his bottle and he drank the whole thing. He's just like a baby."

Jessie chuckled. "When you were a baby, Henry and I used to give you a bottle when you woke us up. *You* always drank the whole thing, too."

As the Aldens walked along, Miss Sayer's van went by. The children waved, but the van didn't slow down. The children could see Chatter Bear's large red head staring straight ahead at the road.

When the Aldens arrived at the toy hospital, a small crowd had gathered around Miss Sayer's van. Everyone wanted to see her talking bear.

"Step back!" Miss Sayer cried, beeping her horn. "Doctor Firman! Oh, Doctor Firman!"

When Doc came out to see what the fuss was about, the Aldens almost didn't recognize him. Instead of his faded blue farm overalls, he was wearing a crisp white doctor's coat and a stethoscope around his neck.

Miss Sayer waved him toward her van. "Doctor Firman. I need you to help Chatter Bear right away. Do you have a stretcher to carry him in?"

"I'm the stretcher." Doc picked up the huge red bear with both arms. "What seems to be the problem?"

"His voice," Miss Sayer told Doc. "It isn't working."

Doc led everyone inside. "Let's put Chatter Bear up on the examining table in here. I'll see what I can do. Please step back, everyone."

"Here, let me remove Chatter Bear's bow," Miss Sayer said. "His voice recorder is in the back of his neck. And he needs new batteries for his eyes. They've been flickering instead of flashing."

Doc noticed the Aldens standing to the side with Mister B., who wasn't flickering or flashing. "You children can go visit my other workroom in back. That's where I keep my special older patients," Doc said with a smile. "There's a book room back there, too, full of bear books."

The Aldens didn't need much coaxing. Old bears were just the kind of bears they liked. They headed straight for the door marked ANTIQUE BEAR DEN.

Inside, shelves and cabinets were filled with old stuffed toys. Scraps of woolly fabrics and woolly fur lay in piles around a large worktable. Off to the side stood several cabinets. Bears that looked even older than Mister B. stared back at the Aldens through the glass cabinet doors.

The children discovered they weren't alone.

A gray-haired woman with a braid wound on top of her head knelt in front of an open cabinet. The Aldens saw her before she saw them.

Jessie coughed to get the woman's attention. "Hello. We're the Aldens."

The woman stood up, surprised. Her rosy cheeks turned even rosier. "What are you doing in Doctor Firman's workroom?" she asked. "He doesn't allow children in here by themselves."

"Sorry if we startled you," Jessie said. "He said it was okay for us to come in here. He's busy fixing a talking bear."

"Hmmf!" the woman said. "Talking bears. What will be next?"

"Oh," Violet said when she noticed the woman was looking at Mister. B. "Would you like to see our bear?"

The woman looked over at Mister B.

"Hmmm. Well, yes, your bear is an old one but not very valuable."

Violet swallowed hard. "He's valuable to us. We love him. He belonged to our grandfather."

The woman nodded, and her voice changed a little. "Ah, I see," she said. "If it belonged to someone in your family, I can see how it would be important to you." She shut the door to the cabinet, turned the key, and walked to the far end of the room as if she couldn't wait to get away from the children.

Jessie stooped down to read a sign on the cabinet the woman had been looking at. " 'Herr Bears.' I wonder what they are. Very old ones, I guess. There's only one of them in this cabinet right now. Let's go look at Doc's bear books, then come back," she whispered to the other children. "That woman keeps staring at us as if she wants us to leave."

In the book room, the Aldens found another surprise visitor. An older man, all by himself, sat in a comfy chair by the bookcases. He seemed so lost in the book on his lap, he didn't look up when the children entered.

"Um, hello," Violet said softly.

The man's pen clattered to the floor along with a notebook.

Violet bent down to pick up the man's things.

"Leave them!" the man said in a gruff voice.

Violet stepped back. "I'm sorry," she said. "We didn't mean to disturb you. I don't like being interrupted, either, when I'm reading or doing my homework."

The man gathered up his notebook, which was jammed with loose papers. "This isn't homework, young lady. May I ask how you got in here? Doctor Firman's library is for grown-ups."

Violet looked around at the many children's books about bears. "There are lots of bear books for children," she said in her most polite voice.

"Nonsense!" the man said. "Well, I guess my peace and quiet has come to an end."

With that, the man put on his brown wool hat and grabbed his walking stick, his notebooks, and an armful of books. He went into the Bear Den and began poking around. Every few minutes he glanced back at the book room as if he couldn't wait for the Aldens to leave.

"I wonder if he's a bear doctor, too," Henry whispered. "Not a very friendly one like Doc, though."

Benny was restless. He liked books, but he liked toys even more. "Can we go back and look at the old bears now?"

Jessie peeked through the door. "We better wait, Benny. Now Miss Sayer is in there with that man. The other woman must have left. I'd rather not have the two of them standing over us while we look at Doc's antique bears. Let's wait until they leave. Then we can go back."

A few minutes later, Jessie checked the Bear Den again. "Okay, now we can look around as much as we like without anybody thinking we shouldn't. Miss Sayer is out front bothering Doc again. I wonder if he figured out how to fix her bear."

"I'mmm Chaaaattter Baaaaar," the Aldens overheard the bear. "Annnnnd IIIII like toooooo talkkkkkk."

Miss Sayer scolded Doc. "You still didn't fix him. Now his voice is too low and too slow. Nobody will be able to understand what he's saying. That's not how he's supposed to talk."

Violet hugged Mister B. He wasn't saying a word.

"Please, Miss Sayer," the children heard Doc say. "I need plenty of light and space to work on Chatter Bear. Why don't you go work on your booth at the Town Hall and come back here later?"

Miss Sayer hesitated before finally leaving Doc and Chatter Bear.

"Whew!" Doc said to the Aldens when they came out to see him. "It's hard to work when someone stands over you."

"Oh, would you like us to leave until you're done?" Jessie asked.

Doc smiled. "Some interruptions I enjoy. How do you like all the antique bears in the Bear Den?"

"I like the one called Herr Bear," Jessie said. "Whose bear is it?"

"The owner, Mrs. Withers, isn't arriving for a few days. That's when the prize is given for the rarest bear in the Teddy Bear Jamboree," said Doc. "Herr bear is so rare that he has a good chance of winning."

Henry thought about this. "Maybe that's why the lady with the braid opened the cabinet to look at it."

Now Doc looked worried. "With the jamboree about to start, so many visitors stopped by, I lost track of who was here. This is why I always keep the Herr Bear cabinet locked. That particular Herr Bear is extremely rare."

"How come?" Benny wanted to know.

"Well," Doc said. "He's the boy twin of a female bear called Fräulein Bear. That means 'Miss Bear' in German; Herr Bear means 'Mister Bear.' The Swiss designer made only one twin pair for his own children. The only difference between them is the color of their eyes. The girl bear has golden eyes and the boy blue eyes. The designer made other Herr Bears, but they have black eyes, and they are smaller than the twins."

"Does the owner own Fräulein Bear, too?" Violet asked Doc. "It's sad when brothers and sisters get separated from each other — especially twins."

"Even if they're bear twins," Benny added.

"I know," Doc agreed. "Unfortunately, no one has been able to track down the girl twin. I've checked all my antique bear books, searched the Internet, and asked every teddy bear collector I've met about Fräulein Bear. No luck so far."

"We didn't get a good look at Herr Bear," Benny said. "The lady closed the cabinet."

"Whew," Doc said, relieved to hear this. "I must have left the key in the lock by mistake when I heard Miss Sayer carrying on before. Well, no harm done. I'll get Herr Bear from the cabinet so you can get a good look at him."

Everyone followed Doc into the Bear Den. When they came to the Herr Bear cabinet, the children stared inside.

Doc's key was still in the lock. But there was no bear staring back. The cabinet was empty.

CHAPTER 3

Hey! Hay!

The next morning after breakfast, the Aldens dressed in their old work clothes. They had important chores to do in the barn. Peggy and Doc had asked them to help with the sheep shearing and said it was a fuzzy, messy job.

"There you go," Jessie said, when she helped Benny untangle his overalls straps. "Now you look like a real shepherd boy. Maybe the sight of you will cheer up Doc. He's pretty upset about the missing Herr Bear."

"I know how to cheer him up, Jessie," Benny said. "We'll just tell him we always find things for people. So I know we can find a bear."

"Thanks," Doc said, when Benny told him this. "Finding that bear would be a big relief. I'll keep searching, but I only have one set of eyes. You children have four sets."

"Plus Mister B. has one," Benny reminded Doc. "That makes four-and-a-half pairs of eyes."

As the children made their way to the barn, a few cars arrived with even more guests.

"Now we're not the only ones staying here with Miss Sayer," Jessie said. "There's her van next to the barn, right where Peggy doesn't want her to park it."

"Did you kids call me?" Miss Sayer screeched when she heard her name. "Doctor Firman isn't letting you in here, is he? You could scare the sheep. They have to be calm when they get sheared, you know."

Jessie tried hard to be friendly. "Peggy invited us to help out."

"Help out?" Miss Sayer cried. "She won't even allow me to help out. What do a bunch of kids know about sheep shearing, anyway?"

"Peggy told Grandfather she's going to teach us how," Benny said.

"Children shearing sheep?" Miss Sayer said angrily. "I've never heard of such a thing!" She turned and stalked away, muttering to herself.

When they entered the barn, the Aldens heard bleats and baas from the Firmans' small flock.

"Hey, Smudge," Benny said when he passed the lamb pen. "I guess you're too little to get a haircut."

Smudge came right up to the chicken wire that enclosed the pen. "Baa!"

"See you later." Benny patted Smudge's warm head. He joined his brother and sisters gathered around Doc and Peggy. Doc was carefully shearing a sheep with electric clippers.

"That's a good girl," Doc crooned, holding Daisy, a large ewe. He gently cradled her head with one arm as he clipped her fleece with the other. Every few seconds he stopped to stroke Daisy's neck or ears, talking to her the whole time. Daisy seemed to melt in Doc's hands while he clipped her.

"Any of you children want to help me with Snowflake?" Doc asked when Daisy scampered off with her new short hairdo. "Just hold him gently while I clip."

Jessie knew what to do right away. "Watch likes it when we stroke him under his chin like this."

Snowflake relaxed in Jessie's arms while Doc finished the haircut. After that, Doc let each of the children take turns holding the ewes and rams during the shearing.

"You Aldens are very good with animals," Doc said when he finished the shearing.

"Look at all this fleece!" Benny cried afterward. The barn floor was covered with huge puffs of fleece. "You could stuff a hundred bears with all this wool, even big gigantic ones like Chatter Bear."

Peggy laughed. "We're not done yet, Benny, not even close," she said. "You can help me carry all this fleece to the skirting table in the next room."

"Is that where you make wool skirts?" Benny asked.

Doc laughed. "It's a special kind of table where we examine the wool. We pull out any parts that are tangled or dirty. Peggy and I need plenty of helpers to carry in all this fleece."

The Aldens each took great heaps of wool in their arms. They carried them into a little room attached to the barn. The puffs were so big, the children looked like sheep themselves.

"Okay, toss an armful on the skirting table," Doc told Henry. "I'll show you how to make sure it's smooth and clean. Peggy only uses the finest fleece to cover her bears. The other clean parts are used for stuffing."

"Save some stuffing for me!" Benny said. He laughed. "That's what I always say at Thanksgiving!"

"Benny means save some stuffing for Mister B.," Violet explained.

"And some for the Herr Bear," Benny said to Doc. "We're going to find him for you."

Doc looked a little worried. "I sure wish you would. If I don't find him soon, I'll need to contact the owner. But I'd like to avoid that if I can."

After Doc left, Peggy showed the Aldens how to sort the wool. The children soon figured out which wool to set aside for spinning and which wool would make good bear stuffing.

"See this pile?" Peggy asked. "It's for Mister B." She patted a big clean puff of fleece. "We'll wash it later to get out some of the oils. After it dries, we can plump up Mister B."

"Mister B. would like that," Violet said. "Thank you for teaching us so much."

Benny looked up at Peggy. "Miss Sayer said kids shouldn't help the sheep get sheared and that she isn't even allowed to do anything."

Peggy bit her lip. "Oh, dear. I do wish she would appreciate that Doc and I have helped her so much over the years with her bear business. But I can't let her in on all my secrets. My Peggy Bears are special because we use wool from our own sheep. Not many teddy bear designers do that."

"Is Miss Sayer a copycat?" Benny asked.

Peggy laughed. "Let's say more like a copybear. She's tried to copy other bears, too. Now she's working on a talking bear, even though there are already talking bears available. Every year, Doc and I try to convince her to design a brand-new kind of bear instead."

"Guess what, Peggy," Benny announced. "We're going to find out who took Doc's missing Herr Bear."

Peggy put down the wool in her hands. "Really? Now, how do you plan to do that?"

"We can keep an eye on people," Benny said. "Like everybody who was in Doc's hospital yesterday. And at the jamboree, we'll see if anyone's snooping around old bears too much."

"Hmmm," Peggy said. "You may get a chance to do that tomorrow. I was hoping you would help me set up my Peggy Bear booth at the Town Hall. Have you any suspects yet?"

Benny looked up at Peggy. "A few, but we're not telling until we catch them."

Peggy sighed. "I see. It would certainly put Doc's mind at rest to find that Herr Bear soon. This mystery has him so upset."

"Don't worry," Benny said. "We like solving mysteries."

Peggy brushed all the wool fuzz from her coveralls and jacket. "Then good luck. Now I hope you don't mind if I leave you for a while. I need to pack the station wagon for the jamboree. You've learned so quickly, I know you can finish up on your own."

The Aldens worked quietly after Peggy left. They wanted to pay close attention and do a good job for Peggy and Doc.

"What's that creaking?" Henry said a few minutes later.

"Hey, who just dropped hay on my head?" Benny asked when he felt some hay land on his hair. He started wiggling and scratching himself. "Some of it went down my neck, too."

When the children looked up, they saw more strands of hay drifting down.

"The wind must have blown open the hayloft door," Jessie said.

"I'll go up and shut it," Henry said. "We have to keep the barn warm for the sheep."

"The ladder is outside," Jessie reminded Henry.

The children followed Henry out. While Jessie held the ladder, Henry climbed up and shut the hayloft door. "There," he said when he came down. "Now we're safe from any more unexpected flying objects."

The children decided to take a short break to visit the sheep in the main part of the barn. Soon they were surrounded by the Firmans' flock with their new short hairdos.

"They like to cuddle with us because we're warm," Jessie said as one sheep after another nudged her and the other children with their noses. "They all want to be stroked and petted."

"Okay, guys, that's enough," Henry told the nuzzling sheep. "We have to get back to work. Stop crying now."

But the sheep didn't stop crying. The Aldens could hear them bleating while they worked.

When Jessie returned to the skirting table, something was missing. "Where's that nice big clean pile of fleece Peggy left for Mister B.? It was right here."

Henry checked under the table. "It's getting weird in here. First the door blows open for no reason. Now some of the fleece we cleaned just disappeared. Pretty strange, if you ask me. Listen, now the dogs are barking outside."

"Maybe they want to come in where it's warm," Violet said.

The children ran out. They found Taf and Midnight growling at Miss Sayer's yellow van.

Henry ran ahead and came back laughing. "Guess what they're barking at? Chatter Bear! Miss Sayer has him in the van, but she can't turn off his voice box. It's pretty funny."

The other children ran over to the van. Chatter Bear's voice wasn't low and slow now but as chirpy and fast as a chipmunk's. "Imchatterbearandiliketotalk."

"Stop that barking!" Miss Sayer told the Firmans' dogs. "Goodness, children, take those dogs away before Chatter Bear gets any more upset. I went over a big bump, and that made his voice box break again."

The Aldens tried hard not to burst out laughing. Instead they clapped and whistled to get the dogs away from Miss Sayer's van. Only they weren't quick enough. Midnight decided he wanted to sniff Chatter Bear and leaped up to the front seat.

"Down! Get down!" Miss Sayer screamed. "Get this dog down before he hurts my bear!"

Jessie ran over and grabbed Midnight's collar. "Come on, Midnight. Let's go for a walk."

Those were the magic words. Midnight backed out of the van. Jessie reached in to straighten out Chatter Bear, who had tipped over sideways. "There," she said after she fastened the seat belt over him. That's when she noticed Miss Sayer's big orange tote bag. Stuffed inside was at least enough clean silky fleece to fill a few nice bears.

CHAPTER 4

Syrup and Suspects

"I smell maple syrup," a voice said from under the covers in Benny's bed.

Jessie sat up and sniffed. "I smell it, too. It must be coming from the sugarhouse. Peggy said that's where they boil the sap from their maple trees to get syrup. Mmm. Maybe this morning we'll get some of those delicious-tasting pancakes Grandfather told us about."

"Baa," the Aldens heard next as they slowly awakened. Smudge looked up from the basket of fleece by Benny's bed. He wanted breakfast, too.

Soon more animal sounds joined the chorus. Rudy the rooster was crowing outside. Midnight and Taf were scratching and whining at the Aldens' door.

"No use trying to sleep any longer," Henry said. "It's a zoo around here. I guess it's time to get up."

In no time, the children had dressed and tidied up Shepherd's Cottage. Animals trailing, they headed toward the main house, where Peggy and Doc's famous Woolly Farm breakfast was being served.

"Oh, look, there goes Miss Sayer with that tote bag of hers," Jessie said. "Now it doesn't looked all bulged out the way it did yesterday. But I still have a feeling she's the one who took the special fleece Peggy set aside."

"Should we ask her?" Benny wanted to know. "If she did take Peggy's fleece, we should tell her to bring it back!"

Jessie hesitated. "I would, but I don't want her to know we're watching her — at least until we find the person who took Doc's Herr Bear."

"I could sit next to her at breakfast and drop a fork or something," Benny said. "Then I could see if there's any fleece sticking out of her pocketbook — or maybe even the Herr Bear."

Henry picked up Benny by both arms and gave him a whirl. "Good plan, Benny. Just don't let Miss Sayer take the bacon and sausages from your plate while you're under the table."

"I won't," Benny said, very certain of that.

The Aldens dropped off Smudge in the lamb pen, then came in the kitchen entrance of the main house. Peggy was at the stove, carefully stacking some golden pancakes onto a plate.

"Mmm. Good morning. Need any help?" Henry asked.

Peggy looked up. "Good morning, children. You're just in time to bring this plate to Professor Tweedy. He's the man at the corner table, with the glasses. Maybe you can keep him company by sitting at his table. He said his pancakes were too dry, so I made him some more."

Benny sniffed the air. "These sure don't look too dry. We were going to sit next to Miss Sayer, though."

Peggy looked over the children's heads. "Oh, she just sat down with some other bear people here for the jamboree. Professor Tweedy is our only guest this week who isn't a teddy bear person." She bent down to whisper to the children. "He's very serious, but I'm sure he would enjoy meeting four polite children."

Jessie looked up at Peggy. "Oh, we already met him at the toy hospital," she whispered back. "He didn't seem to think we belonged there."

Peggy put down her measuring cup. "Professor Tweedy at the toy hospital? Doc didn't mention that. I'm surprised. The professor usually avoids bear people." Peggy dropped a pat of butter on the pancakes. "He told me he's giving an important talk on American presidents at a nearby college.

He checked in late last night, so Doc hasn't seen him here yet."

"There were a lot of people at the toy hospital," Jessie mentioned. "That man was in the book room reading. Then we saw him looking around the Bear Den. I'm sure it's the same man."

Peggy's eyebrows went up in surprise. "Goodness. You just never know about people."

When the Aldens joined Professor Tweedy in the dining room, he didn't look up from his magazine. He frowned as the children sat down.

"Peggy asked us to give you these," Violet said when she set his pancakes on the table. "We're the Aldens. We saw you at Doc's toy hospital, remember?"

The professor finally peered over the glasses perched on his nose. He didn't seem too interested in the four pairs of eyes staring at him. "Indeed." Then he went back to stirring his coffee and reading his magazine, as if the children weren't even there.

"We're here for the Teddy Bear Jam-

boree," Violet said. "It's going to be fun. We have a bear we're going to fix up. Want to see him?"

Mr. Tweedy speared a bite of pancake, ignoring Violet.

"Our bear is almost as old as our grandfather," Violet said.

Professor Tweedy finally tore himself away from his pancakes and his magazine when he heard this. "Well, what year was it made? Where did it come from? What kind of bear is it?"

"The nice old kind," Violet said in her soft, polite voice. "The kind we cuddle when we get sick or play with when we're lonesome."

The professor sniffed. "I don't mean that! I mean where is this bear of yours from? What brand is it? Goodness, young lady, don't you know anything about your bear's history? If it's an old bear, you should be taking care of it. The bear isn't supposed to take care of you!"

When Benny heard this, he just had to say something. "We do take care of him.

We're going to help fix him up and everything."

"That's an expert's job," Professor Tweedy said. "Certainly *not* a job for children."

Miss Sayer finally livened up the Aldens' table a few minutes later. "Hello, I'm Hazel Sayer," she said to the professor. "May I borrow the sugar bowl from this table? Are you a bear collector? I saw you at Doctor Firman's hospital. Are you a seller or a buyer?"

"Neither," Professor Tweedy said.

This didn't stop Miss Sayer. She was as chatty as her own talking bear when it came to bears.

"What's that you're reading?" she asked, trying to get a closer look.

Mr. Tweedy closed the magazine partway. "A history magazine."

Benny had been peeking at the professor's magazine, too. "Wow, that looks like a fun history magazine, since it has all those toys in it."

Professor Tweedy rolled up the magazine

and stuffed it in the briefcase he carried everywhere. "It's not a child's magazine. Now, if you wouldn't mind, I'd like to finish my breakfast. Talking while dining is bad for one's stomach. And I have quite a bit of reading to do."

Even Miss Sayer looked hurt when she heard this. She returned to her table without the sugar bowl.

The Aldens finished breakfast and didn't dare speak to Professor Tweedy again. They decided to bring their own dishes into the kitchen to save Peggy from the extra work.

"Well, did you melt the professor's heart?" Peggy asked with a twinkle in her eye.

"I don't think so," Jessie answered when she put her dish down. She told Peggy what the professor had said. "He even scolded Violet about not taking good care of Mister B."

"Goodness, how did that come up?" Peggy asked.

"When I mentioned to him that we'd seen him at the toy hospital," Violet said.

"He asked a lot of questions after I said we had an old bear."

Peggy looked at her watch. "Well, I'm sorry you kids didn't have such a great breakfast. But you can still have a great day. You know, if you go over to the Town Hall now, I think you could work on my Peggy Bears booth. That would give me some time to wash and dry the other fleece I found for Mister B. After all, you want him to look handsome for the Best Bears Contest at the end of the jamboree."

"And maybe win, even if Mister B. doesn't know how to talk," Benny said.

"Most of the best bears don't talk — at least not with voices," Peggy said. "They speak to us in their own way, just by being bears. Now, here's the list of things to do when you get to the Town Hall. I left everything you'll need in my space there — Row Eleven, Booth E. Give me a call if you have any questions."

"I have a lot of questions," Henry said after they left Peggy. "Why would somebody like Professor Tweedy, with no interest in bears, go to Doc's toy hospital? And why would he ask us all about Mister B.?"

"Or lie about reading a magazine? I really think that magazine was about toys, not history," Jessie added. "Let's make sure to keep an eye on Professor Tweedy as well as Miss Sayer."

"Mister B. can only keep one eye on them," Benny reminded everyone. "That's 'cause he's only got one eye!"

CHAPTER 5

Bears Everywhere

When the Aldens arrived, the Old Mills Town Hall was buzzing with bear people. They carried big bears, little bears, and in-between bears. Some were unpacking bear music boxes; others bear T-shirts, bear books, and every kind of bear knickknack.

The Teddy Bear Jamboree was nearly under way.

"Let's get our badges," Jessie said. She soon found the blue badges Peggy had arranged for them ahead of time.

"We belong to Peggy Bears," Benny said when a security guard stopped the Aldens at the entrance.

The man winked at the older children. "You can go in, young man, but no growling."

"Only my stomach growls at lunchtime," Benny said.

The man laughed, then waved them in.

People were swarming all over. The children looked for the row where Peggy told them she had left her things.

"*Eleven E*. Oh, good," Henry said when he found the right row. "Peggy has one of the best spots. It's right near the entrance. That way everyone will see it."

The shelves, lights, signs — and boxes of Peggy Bears, of course — were piled up, ready for the Alden touch.

Jessie took an envelope from her backpack. "Peggy put in a note saying we can fix up the booth any way we want. Here are photographs from last year's booth. See how great it looked?"

"Oh, they're so cute," Violet said when

she saw pictures of fuzzy Peggy Bears lined up on shelves the year before. "I love her bears best. Most of them are the same color as the sheep — not dyed red or purple or strange colors that animals don't have. I wish we could open her bear boxes right now."

"Not yet," Jessie advised. "We need to put the shelves and tables together first. Here's Doc's toolbox."

Soon the Aldens were busy hammering in nails and putting up shelves for the display. A couple rows away, they heard a recording of "The Teddy Bears' Picnic," so they hummed along as they worked. It didn't feel like work at all.

A few minutes later, loud voices nearby interrupted these happy sounds. One of the voices belonged to the woman they'd seen at Doc's.

"I must switch my location immediately," the woman was saying. "I cannot have a successful booth with all these children running about."

"Now, now, Mrs. Keppel," the security

guard said to the woman. "These children are good friends of Peggy Firman. She told me herself they are quite responsible. Why, just look at the job they've done on the booth already."

The woman pushed back a loose strand of hair from the old-fashioned braid on her head. Staring at the guard, she didn't seem about to give in. "How will there be room for my customers with these children nearby? After all, my Woodland Bears are very delicate."

Violet put down her hammer and went over to the woman. "Hello, I'm Violet Alden. We met at Doctor Firman's Toy Hospital. I love Woodland Bears. My aunt Jane sends me one for every birthday. Now I have a whole collection. I haven't broken a single one. I even take them down from the shelf to dust them once a week. I think they're wonderful."

Violet's voice seemed to calm down the woman. "Well, then. Do you wash them regularly with baby soap and dry them with soft flannel?" the woman asked.

"Yes," Violet answered. "Once a month, I give them a bath in warm, soapy water, just like it says on your little booklets. Do you need help unpacking all your boxes? It probably takes longer to set up little china bears than Peggy Bears."

The woman seemed about to say yes, then changed her mind. "No. I . . . I can't have anyone else handling my bears. Especially not children."

By this time, the security guard came by again. "Everything okay now, Mrs. Keppel?"

"*Ja*," Mrs. Keppel answered.

Benny took his head out of a box of Peggy Bears. He whispered in Violet's ear, "Mrs. Keppel sounded just like Mr. Walder, down the street near Grandfather's house."

"I know," Violet whispered back. "I think she's from Europe, just like Mr. Walder. That's where Woodland Bears are made."

When the Peggy Bear booth was done, other bear sellers came by to admire the Aldens' work.

Soon Benny's stomach began to growl, just like he'd told the security man. "It must be time for lunch."

Jessie checked her watch. "Almost. Oh, there's Peggy. She's taking us to lunch, remember?"

Peggy lit up with smiles when she saw the way the Aldens had fixed up her booth. "You children certainly have the right touch," she said, looking around. "I never thought to put the little bears in the laps of the bigger bears. I might even sell them as a set. What a clever idea. I love it!"

"Thanks." Henry folded the stepladder and placed it behind the display. "With four of us working, we got a lot done." He lowered his voice and nodded toward Mrs. Keppel in the next booth. "At first that lady didn't want us here. Then she was nice after she found out Violet has a Woodland Bear collection."

Peggy's eyes widened. "Oh, how lucky that my booth is next to hers." Peggy walked over to Mrs. Keppel. "Hello. I'm

Peggy Firman of Peggy Bears. I'm delighted our booths are side by side. We've never had Woodland Bears at the jamboree. Did you bring them all the way from Europe?"

"*Ja*," Mrs. Keppel said. "I mean, no. Well, I must finish my work. Farewell." Mrs. Keppel turned away.

The Aldens bundled up a few boxes, dusted shelves, and swept the booth. They put up the velvet rope so no one would come inside the booth while they were gone.

An announcement came over the loudspeakers: "The delivery truck has just arrived. Would the following people please come to the back of the auditorium to pick up your shipments? Benson, Davis, Firman, Hudson, Keppel, Laramie, Richman, and Sayer. Please pick up your deliveries at the back of the room."

"Don't you want to come with me?" Peggy asked Mrs. Keppel.

"*Nein*," Mrs. Keppel answered. "I mean, no."

After Peggy left, Mrs. Keppel looked at the Aldens.

"Do not touch anything here," Mrs. Keppel said. "I know how children are. It is very tempting to take things that don't belong to you."

Jessie felt her heart thump. "We wouldn't ever do that, Mrs. Keppel. You don't have to worry."

Mrs. Keppel's pale skin reddened with shame. She almost seemed about to apologize to the Aldens. Instead, she turned on the heels of her old-fashioned shoes and went off to get her packages.

"I wish I could figure her out," Violet said. "Sometimes she starts to like us, then she doesn't."

Benny moved over to the farthest side of Peggy's booth, then stretched his neck over to Mrs. Keppel's booth. "I don't even like china stuff." He hoped she had something he did like. "Hey, come here. Look at those furry brown ears sticking out from a bag under one of the shelves. See?"

The other children came over for a look.

They were careful not to put one finger or toe into Mrs. Keppel's booth.

"Good eyes, Benny," Henry said. "But I can't see enough of the rest of it to tell what kind of bear that is."

"The furry old kind," Benny said.

CHAPTER 6

Big, Fuzzy Heads

On the way to lunch, the Aldens told Peggy about Mrs. Keppel and the furry ears.

"I couldn't tell if they were Herr Bear ears," Benny said. "But you know what? They sure weren't made out of china stuff like those other bears she has."

"I almost asked her about the Herr Bear again to see if she would get nervous," Henry said. "Then the newspaper photographer showed up to take pictures. That seemed to upset her."

"How odd," Peggy said. "Do you believe she took the Herr Bear?"

Before the others could answer, Violet spoke up. "We saw her put the bear back and lock the cabinet. Woodland Bears are special. I don't think someone who makes them could be a thief."

Benny disagreed. "Who would want small china bears that you have to dust and everything? You could have a cuddly bear that doesn't need dusting."

"There's one way to find out," Violet said. "We'll have to go back and talk to her more. I'd like to get to know Mrs. Keppel better, anyway."

By this time, Peggy and the Aldens had arrived in front of the town restaurant.

Peggy felt for something in her pocket. "Oh, dear. I think I left my keys on the table in the booth. Would one of you run back and get them for me?"

"I'll go," Henry said before sprinting off.

"Bring Mister B. back," Benny called out to Henry. "I hid him under the table. I sure don't want him to get lost like the Herr Bear did."

Henry made his way through the crowds. When he came to Peggy's booth, he spotted her keys right away. "There they are," he said, dropping them into the pocket of his jeans. Then he bent down to reach for Mister B.

A familiar pair of green mud boots was sticking out from under the table!

"Miss Sayer!" Henry said when he realized who was wearing the boots. "What are you doing under there?"

"What am I doing?" Miss Sayer grabbed her orange tote bag. "What are you doing with a blue badge? Those are only for bear sellers, not customers and children."

Henry held the badge out for Miss Sayer to read. "See? We're Peggy's assistants. That's how we got our badges. Did you come to help her, too?"

Miss Sayer seemed annoyed at Henry's question. "Of course not. I have my own seller's badge, as you can see. However,

Peggy said I could borrow things I needed for my booth. I was looking for . . . for gift boxes."

Henry looked down. Something with Peggy's name on it was sticking out of Miss Sayer's tote bag.

"Were you planning to tell her about taking her pattern book?" a voice nearby said. It was Mrs. Keppel, and she was frowning at Miss Sayer.

Miss Sayer looked away from the woman. "I . . . well, it was dark under there. How was I supposed to tell a book from a box?" Miss Sayer shoved Peggy's pattern book back under the table. She quickly gathered up her things and left.

"Thanks," Henry told Mrs. Keppel. "I'm glad she didn't take Peggy's keys, too. I'm Henry Alden."

"I'm Elsa." Mrs. Keppel almost smiled, but not quite. "Elsa Keppel. Don't leave important things lying about. You must be careful about thieves."

"We try to be," Henry said. "This is what

I was looking for," he said when he reached under the table and found Mister B. "So long." Henry quickly glanced into Mrs. Keppel's booth. There was nothing but china bears to be seen — no furry ears at all.

Henry left the hall, eager to tell Peggy and his brother and sisters about Miss Sayer and Mrs. Keppel. When he stepped outside, he saw a crowd of children and their parents. As he drew closer, he discovered what everyone was looking at — three furry bear characters mingling in the crowd.

Henry saw Peggy on the far side of the crowd and called out to her. "Hey, Peggy," Henry said. "Where are my sisters and Benny? They'd sure like to see these bears, too."

Peggy put her hand over her mouth to cover a grin.

"What's up?" Henry asked when he reached her. "Did they go inside already?"

That's when the shortest bear came up to Henry and began to giggle.

"Hey, I know that laugh!" Henry bent down to get a closer look at the bear. "That's you inside there, isn't it, Benny?" he whispered at the bear's big furry head.

The bear laughed again. "See, I told you we could fool him!" It was Benny's voice. "And guess what, Henry. Jessie and Violet are bears, too!"

Peggy laughed, then guided the three bears into the restaurant. They scampered off to the rest rooms to change.

"I hope you like a good joke," Peggy said to Henry. "Every year, the people who run the jamboree have three children dress up as the three bears from *Goldilocks and the Three Bears*. I hope you don't mind that I volunteered Benny and your sisters for the job. They're just the right size for the costumes. Jessie is the Papa Bear, Violet the Mama Bear. Benny is the Baby Bear, of course. It was his idea to fool you when you came back."

"You rascal!" Henry said when Benny came back as a boy and not a bear. "You sure had me fooled. Now, here's a real bear for you — a stuffed one anyway." He handed over Mister B. "And here are your keys, Peggy, they were right where you thought you left them."

"Know what, Henry?" Benny asked. "When we have those costumes on, we can walk around and search for the Herr Bear. Nobody will know it's us."

"Good plan," Henry agreed. "Now let's find a booth — a restaurant booth that sells sandwiches, not bears. I'm hungry. What are you going to have?" he asked his brother and sisters.

"Honey!" they all said at the same time.

"Miss Sayer had one of your pattern books in her tote bag," Henry told Peggy before he even looked at the menu. "Mrs. Keppel told her to put it back."

Peggy sighed. "Oh, dear. That may be my fault. This morning I told Miss Sayer that if she needed anything, she could help herself to supplies from my booth. I didn't mean my pattern book, though. I thought she would know better than that."

"Did she put it back?" Benny asked before deciding on a grilled cheese sandwich.

"She sure did," Henry said. "We've got enough to look for. We'll be plenty busy searching for the Herr Bear and the person who took it."

"Starting right after lunch," Jessie told Peggy. "Unless you have plans for us."

Peggy looked up from her menu. "Well, I was hoping you children could help me and Doc do some bear repairs at the toy hospital."

The children wanted to be in two places at the same time.

Then Jessie figured out a way they could be. "I know. We need to find out more reasons someone might want to steal the Herr Bear. Didn't Doc say he has lots of books about collectible bears? We could get information and maybe even search on the computer at the toy hospital. Would that be okay, Peggy?"

"Of course," Peggy said. "At the same time, you could take turns helping stuff and sew up the last of my Peggy Bears — along with Mister B., of course."

"Hey," Benny said. "Look who just walked by."

"Professor Tweedy." Henry swiveled around to see where the professor was headed. "He's two booths back."

"Then that's where I'm going," Jessie said. "Our napkin dispenser is empty. I'll get some napkins from Professor Tweedy's booth and see what he's up to. He's got that big briefcase he always carries everywhere. I wonder what he's doing here."

Jessie waited a few minutes, then got up. The other children pretended to eat their food. They glanced up every few seconds to see what Jessie was going to do.

When she came to Professor Tweedy's booth, Jessie saw his open briefcase on the seat. She was disappointed there was no bear inside. In front of him, the professor had spread out his notebook, some papers, and a magazine opened to bear photographs. He was copying something into his notebook.

"Oh, hi, Professor Tweedy," Jessie said, not hesitating a bit. "I'd like a few napkins from that dispenser," she said before the professor had a chance to protest. "The one at our booth is empty. Thanks so much. See you later."

Jessie scooted back to her own booth with a fistful of napkins. "Guess what. Professor Tweedy didn't have the Herr Bear, but he was definitely taking down notes about bears. I saw it for sure."

"Then for sure we're going to find out why," Henry said before biting down on his double-decker turkey sandwich.

CHAPTER 7

Too Many Bears

When the Aldens strolled over to the toy hospital after lunch, the CLOSED sign was posted on the door.

"Don't worry," Peggy said. "Doc closed early. He needs to finish all the work he has on the bears people dropped off for the jamboree. He told me he'll be in the workshop."

Peggy and the children walked around the back. They were surprised to see Miss Sayer's yellow van backing out. The passenger with the familiar red furry head wasn't in the van.

"Oh, dear, Chatter Bear must be inside," Peggy said. "That must mean Doc is working on him again. He fixed him as best he could. Finally he told Miss Sayer her bear is far from ready to be presented."

Peggy unlocked the back door for the Aldens. When they stepped inside, Chatter Bear lay on the worktable.

Doc was bent over him, adjusting some buttons. "Oh, thank goodness you're here, everybody. I could sure use some help. Miss Sayer said this fellow now talks when she doesn't want him to and won't speak when she does want him to. I've spent more time on this patient than all my other ones put together."

"That's why we came over," Jessie said. "Peggy's going to show us how to fix some of the bears."

"The children also want to find out more about Herr Bears," Peggy said. "I'm letting them use our computer to get the information they're looking for."

"Even bear detectives use computers," Benny told Doc.

Chatter Bear continued to stare at the ceiling. For once, he had nothing to say. Doc had taken out all his batteries. "I found it too strange having his eyes blink at me while I worked on his voice box," Doc explained. "Oh, one more problem. You know that pile of old bear-collector magazines we were going to try to sell, Peggy? Now some of those are gone, too."

"Lots of things are walking out of the toy hospital," Peggy said. "Not just bears."

"I'm almost afraid to ask, but did you children have any luck tracking down Herr Bear?" Doc asked. "His owner gets here tomorrow afternoon. I don't even want to think about telling her he disappeared. I could try tracking down another one, but it won't be the same."

Benny touched Chatter Bear's red nylon ears. "We saw some brown furry ears sticking out of Mrs. Keppel's bag. Only we couldn't tell if they were Herr Bear's ears."

Doc snapped some batteries into Chatter Bear's voice box. "Is Mrs. Keppel that lady who was here the morning you children arrived? With the gray hair in a braid? I never had a chance to help her with her bear. Now I wonder what she wanted."

"What bear?" Jessie asked.

"She had a bear in a blue bag, if I remember correctly," Doc said. "I thought she left after that, but I guess she waited for me in the Bear Den."

"That's when we saw her," Henry said. "I wonder if the bear she brought you was the one Benny saw in her booth."

Doc was done. He pressed a button, and Chatter Bear began to speak: "I'mmm Chaaaattter Baaaaar. Annnnnd IIIII like toooooo talkkkkkk."

The children covered their ears until Doc turned off the bear.

"Can I put the eye batteries in?" Benny asked Doc.

Doc smiled. "Sure. Then you can help me look for a glass eye for Mister B. How's that sound?"

"Like a good idea," Benny said. "Now it's

Mister B.'s turn to see the doctor." After he got Chatter Bear's eyes flashing again, he went off with Doc.

Peggy brought the other children back into the office where the computer was. She clicked the computer mouse a few times. "Here's a list of our favorite places on the Internet for finding information about stuffed bears."

"Thanks," Jessie said. "We're going to look up Professor Tweedy's name and Mrs. Keppel's and Miss Sayer's, too. Maybe we can find some clues about them."

Peggy laughed and clicked on another list. "The professor has probably written a few articles about the presidents for his college. If you type in his name on any of these places, perhaps you can learn more about him. I don't know about the other two people, though. They're not well-known, except to us, of course."

"Thanks, Peggy," Jessie said. "After I finish with the computer, I'll come back and help you with your bears."

After watching Jessie work for a few minutes, Henry and Violet decided to go back to the workroom. They found Doc and Benny sifting through small drawers of glass eyes.

"Here's one that's just right!" Benny cried when he found a golden glass eye for Mister B.

"A perfect match," Doc said. "Let's set it aside. After you kids make a new covering for him, we can attach this new eye and his old one."

Peggy showed the three interested children how to slip off Mister B.'s old wool coat. Then she helped them take it apart to use as a pattern to cut pieces for a new wool covering.

"He looks so sad and pale now, lying there in his thin lining with no nose, or eyes, or mouth," Violet said a few minutes later.

"He looks like a ghost bear," Henry said as he carefully traced a pattern on some stiff paper from the outline of Mister B.'s old wool cover. "Here, Violet. Why don't you cut the pieces now? You have steady hands."

For the next hour, the two older children cut and trimmed and stitched a new woolly cover for Mister B.

"While you two are stitching, I'm going to have Benny stuff Mister B.," Peggy said. "I did manage to find some grade-A fleece. Goodness knows what happened to the fleece we sheared in the barn."

The children worked quietly, stuffing, sewing, threading, and snipping. They only stopped when they heard Jessie call them into the office.

"Come here!" she cried. "You won't believe what I found out about Professor Tweedy."

Henry sat down next to Jessie and began to read the computer screen.

"Skip to the last paragraph in this article about him," Jessie said. "The rest is about some kind of special history project he's working on."

Henry read the last paragraph aloud:

> "*Professor Tweedy's hobbies include bird-watching, stamp collecting, and rare-book*

collecting. For this article, his wife reported that he has also become an expert on antique bears. When asked about this unlikely hobby for a professor of historical research on presidents, all Professor Tweedy would say is, 'Indeed!' "

"Wow!" Benny said. "Now he sounds like someone who might want Herr Bear."

Jessie handed Henry a few sheets of paper that she had printed out. "Maybe, maybe not. Here's an article about Herr Bears that I found on the computer when I looked up antique bears. And guess the name of the daughter of the man who designed the Herr Bear twins. Just guess."

The other children could hardly stand it.

"Is it Miss Sayer's first name?" Benny asked.

"Hazel?" Violet guessed.

Jessie shook her head from side to side. "*Nein!*" she said. "That means 'no' in German. The designer's daughter's name is Elsa. That's Mrs. Keppel's first name."

Peggy looked over Henry's shoulder to read the sheet of paper. "Elsa *Berne*."

"Maybe *Berne* was Mrs. Keppel's name before she got married," Henry said. "The article says another child's name was Kurt Berne, but he died about thirty years ago."

Jessie sank back in her chair. "I couldn't find anything about Elsa Keppel or Hazel Sayer. But I learned a lot about Herr Bears. Some of it is sad. Herr Bears were the most popular bears in Europe a long time ago. They stopped being made after the factory burned down."

"It did?" Violet said. "How awful."

"Yes," Jessie went on, "that made Fritz Berne, the designer, lose his business. I even found an article from an old newspaper about the fire and how the Bernes had to sell their house and almost everything they owned."

Violet was curious about this sad end to the Herr Bears. "Did you find out anything about the twin bears, Jessie?"

"That's the saddest part," Jessie said. "In

the article about the fire, it mentioned that some of the family's things were stolen around the time the Bernes moved away. But no one was ever caught. Apparently the twin bears either disappeared or were stolen."

"You mean Doc's Herr Bear could've been stolen before?" Benny asked.

"Looks like it," Jessie said. "The twin Herr Bears were valuable even back then. Fritz Berne used pictures of them in his advertisements and everything. The bears were famous."

"That's so sad," Violet said. "If Mrs. Keppel is related to Fritz Berne, maybe the Herr Bear is hers. I wonder how we can find out."

The Aldens grew quiet now. Stories about children separated from their homes always made them think about when they left their own home after their mother and father died.

Violet went back to the workroom. She brought something for Jessie. "Look!" she told her sister. "This will cheer you up."

"Mister B.!" Jessie broke into a huge smile. "You have a new covering. Or you almost have a new cover anyway. Plus, you look as if you've been eating too many blueberries. You're nice and chubby now. Grandfather isn't going to recognize you. You're almost as good as new."

Just as the other children began to explain how they had fixed Mister B., they heard a loud thud in the book room. Everyone ran over at once.

"Professor Tweedy!" Peggy said. "What are you doing up there? Please come down."

Professor Tweedy was tottering on a step stool and looking very confused. Above him stood a bookcase with a half-empty shelf. On the floor lay a pile of books.

A large picture book rested on top of the heap. The title said: *Antique Bears*.

CHAPTER 8

Bears on Parade

Benny clicked the seat belt over his furry stomach. "Now Chatter Bear isn't the only bear wearing a seat belt," he announced to everyone in Peggy's car. "Are you sure Miss Sayer and Professor Tweedy didn't see us in our costumes?"

Peggy couldn't help smiling at the sight of the two furry heads in the rearview mirror and the one next to her in the front seat. "I'm sure, Benny," she answered, starting the car. "Miss Sayer left early without even eating any breakfast. She wanted to get the best position in the Teddy Bear Parade."

"What about Professor Tweedy?" Violet asked from inside her Mama Bear costume. "If we see him, we don't want him to know it's us."

"I'm not sure where the professor went," Peggy said, "but he left an hour ago. Don't worry about being in costume. It's our secret. I'll drop you off just outside town, so no one sees that we're together. Oh, here comes Henry on Doc's old bike."

Benny rolled down the window with one paw to talk to Henry. "Make sure Mister B. waves to people watching the parade."

"I will." Henry settled Mister B. into a basket on the handlebars. "Mister B. and I will both wave. Since you guys are in costume, make sure to look for me if you see anything suspicious going on, okay?"

"We will," the three bears said before Peggy pulled away.

A few minutes later, Peggy dropped the children off a couple blocks from the Old Mills Town Hall. Minutes after that, Henry rolled by on the bike. He squeezed the squawky bike horn. The three bears waved back but didn't say anything. They didn't want anyone to know that they had a human brother.

Old Mills looked like a bear town, not a people town. There seemed to be more bear marchers lined in the parade than parade watchers on the sidewalks. Some of the marchers showed off their bears on handmade floats or carts. Others borrowed strollers and wagons to display their favorite bears.

Henry joined the bike marchers. While he waited for the parade to start, he kept an eye on his brother and sisters in their bear costumes. They were surrounded by children who wanted to have their pictures taken with the Three Bears.

Soon a television crew from a news station came by. Jessie, Violet, and Benny were going to be on television. Of course, no one would know who they were, but Henry knew they wouldn't mind!

With crowds surrounding them, the younger Aldens didn't see Mrs. Keppel slip away from the crowd. She stopped to speak to someone standing beside her cart of Woodland Bears. After quickly looking around, she stepped inside the Town Hall.

Henry couldn't believe it. Didn't she know the parade was about to start? He had no choice. He tied up his bike and grabbed Mister B. At the edge of the crowd, he waved his arms at Jessie.

Jessie knew right away that Henry needed her. She whispered to Violet and went off to see what Henry wanted.

"What's the matter, Henry?" Jessie whispered from under her Papa Bear head. She kept on nodding to the crowds while she waited for Henry's answer.

Henry handed her a piece of paper and a pencil. "Could you autograph this for my little brother?" he said. "He likes the story of *Goldilocks and the Three Bears.*"

When Jessie looked down, she saw that Henry had written a message to her:

Mrs. Keppel went into the Town Hall. Let's follow her.

Jessie quickly returned to Benny and Violet. "Stay here," she whispered. "Henry and I have to follow Mrs. Keppel. I'll be back in a while."

Benny wanted to come, but so many children crowded around, he and Violet couldn't get away.

By the time Jessie caught up with Henry, he was already in the lobby. Mrs. Keppel was about ten feet ahead, clicking her thick heels along the marble floors. Tiptoeing behind Mrs. Keppel, Henry and Jessie tried not to sneeze or cough or bump into anything.

Mrs. Keppel turned around a couple times. When she did, the children hid behind the pillars, which were just barely wide enough to hide Jessie's bear head.

Mrs. Keppel entered the main hall, which was dark.

Tiptoeing behind, Henry and Jessie could barely see Mrs. Keppel.

Henry guessed she was headed for her booth. Taking a chance, he signaled to

Jessie to scoot around in another direction.

Jessie made a loop around the other aisles. She and Henry just had to get to Peggy's booth before Mrs. Keppel got to hers.

"I'm glad we wore sneakers," Jessie whispered when they got to Peggy's booth ahead of Mrs. Keppel. She pulled the curtain slightly, just enough to see into Mrs. Keppel's booth. Soon they heard her footsteps. They were afraid to breathe.

Mrs. Keppel turned on the small spotlight in her booth. She took out a key and opened a small wooden cabinet. She pulled out a bag — the very one Benny and Henry had seen. The ears were still sticking out of the bag.

A minute later, the whole bear was sticking out. In fact, an entire Herr Bear was sticking out! Mrs. Keppel picked him up and hugged him. She turned off the light, then left the hall.

"Violet is going to be so upset," Jessie whispered to Henry, feeling upset herself.

"So the thief turned out to be Mrs. Keppel after all. I wonder if she's going to march in the parade with the Herr Bear."

Henry thought about this as he made his way with Jessie through the dark hall. "How can she do that? Doc could have her arrested for theft. Something doesn't make sense."

The children squinted when they came out into the sunlight again. The Teddy Bear Parade was under way. That's when Henry and Jessie noticed two furry marchers going the wrong way.

"You won't believe what we saw!" Jessie said when she and Henry joined Violet and Benny. She forgot all about pretending to be a bear.

Mama Bear's head drooped when she heard what Jessie had to say. "It *was* Mrs. Keppel who took Herr Bear," Violet said. Her Mama Bear costume had a happy bear face, but the voice inside it sounded sad. "I can't believe she was the thief."

"I know," Jessie said. "Look. The parade just stopped so the oompah band can play

a song in front of the mayor. Let's catch up with Mrs. Keppel."

Henry took Mister B. back to his bike while the younger children ran ahead like a trio of bears running through the woods.

"There's the Woodland Bears cart," Violet said when she saw the pretty painted cart a few feet ahead.

The Three Bears surrounded the cart.

"Hello, bears," Mrs. Keppel said cheerfully. "Come meet my bear."

By this time Henry had rolled up on his bike and stopped in front of Mrs. Keppel, too.

"We already met your bear," he said firmly. "Only it's not your bear. That's the Herr Bear that was in Doc Firman's Toy Hospital."

Mrs. Keppel's mouth opened, but nothing came out right away. Finally she found her voice. "You know nothing about this bear. Go find Doctor Firman. I can prove that this bear belongs to me. Can he and the owner say the same about their Herr Bear?"

At that moment, a tuba sounded, and the parade began to move ahead quickly. Mrs. Keppel put her bear over her shoulder and pushed her cart forward. The Aldens dropped back from the marchers.

"I'm really confused," Jessie said. "She made it sound as if that Herr Bear is different than the one we saw at Doc's. Peggy and Doc should be marching by soon."

"There they are!" Benny shouted when he saw the Firmans pushing the Woolly Farm wheelbarrow full of Peggy's fleecy bears. Tucked in back was the basket of fleece from Shepherd's Cottage. "Smudge is in the parade. See?"

Indeed, Smudge was nibbling away on a flowerpot filled with brand-new shoots of green grass.

"Here we are!" Jessie called out before she and the other children stepped into the parade with the Firmans.

"Don't you children look wonderful!" Peggy declared. "We were searching all over for you."

"We were searching all over for your

Herr Bear," Henry announced. "And we found him!"

Doc stopped in place, nearly toppling the wheelbarrow. "What do you mean?"

"Mrs. Keppel took him," Jessie said. "See, up ahead?"

Doc squinted. Mrs. Keppel's bear flopped over her shoulder just like a baby. "It's the Herr Bear, all right," Doc said. "Let's not let them out of our sight. The parade is swinging around to the Town Hall again. Let's stop Mrs. Keppel and get to the bottom of this."

When the Teddy Bear Parade finally broke up, Mrs. Keppel didn't seem surprised to see the Aldens or the Firmans.

Doc stepped in front of Mrs. Keppel. "I need to take a look at the bear you're holding. I have reason to believe it may be the one that disappeared from my toy hospital earlier this week."

The children were surprised that Mrs. Keppel didn't try to get away. In fact, she willingly turned her bear around so Doc could get a better look at it.

Now it was Doc's turn to look surprised. "Your bear has golden eyes, not blue. It's Fräulein Bear."

Mrs. Keppel smiled, but she did not look happy. "Yes, and I possess her birth certificate. Can you say the same for Herr Bear, Doctor Firman?"

CHAPTER 9

Bear Talk

The tubas stopped playing, the marchers stopped marching. But the Aldens didn't stop looking for Herr Bear.

"I'm sad Herr Bear is still missing," Violet said when the doors to the Old Mills Town Hall opened to the public. "But I'm glad Mrs. Keppel didn't take him."

Jessie wasn't quite so sure. "She does have the birth certificate for her Fräulein Bear, but she wouldn't tell Doc anything else. I still think she's hiding something. I just have a feeling she's connected to Herr Bear somehow."

Henry was used to talking to bears now, but he wasn't used to constantly sharing his sisters and brother. Wherever they went in their Three Bears costumes, people followed them.

"I thought we were supposed to follow people, not the other way around," Benny said when he was alone for a minute with Henry. "I like being a bear, but I like being a detective better."

As the children decided what to do next, they heard a familiar voice.

"Ugh, I hear Chatter Bear's voice in the next aisle!" Jessie said. "He's so loud, he drowns out 'The Teddy Bears' Picnic' song. I suppose we ought to visit Miss Sayer's booth. I wonder whether she's having any success with her talking bear."

So the Three Bears, along with their human brother, Henry, followed the sound of Chatter Bear's voice until they came to Miss Sayer's booth.

"What's her bear saying, anyway?" Benny asked. "It's different than before."

As the children drew closer, they made out the words of Chatter Bear's new message: "Come see Sayer's All-Natural Cubs. Come see Sayer's All-Natural Cubs."

Miss Sayer's booth was packed with people who had answered Chatter Bear's invitation.

Henry whispered to the younger children. "Listen, I'll be in the next booth. Since Miss Sayer doesn't know who you are, one of you can ask her a lot of questions while the other two of you look around. Peggy said she's always copying other bears. Maybe the Herr Bear will turn up in Miss Sayer's booth."

Jessie looked at Henry through the eye openings of her costume. "I'd also like to find out if she took all that nice fleece that disappeared from the Firmans' barn. Okay, bears, let's go." She took hold of Benny's paw in one hand and Violet's in the other.

"Oh, no!" Jessie said when she finally got a good look at Miss Sayer's booth.

Violet touched Jessie's arm with her paw. "What's the matter?"

Jessie held out her paw. "Look! Those are copies of Peggy Bears."

The Three Bears stared at the many bears on the shelves. Sure enough, there was a row of stuffed bears that looked almost the same as Peggy's.

"They're not as nice," Violet whispered to Jessie. "Some of the stitching is loose. They're not as plump, either."

Jessie was mad. "So this is why she kept snooping around Doc Firman's Toy Hospital and Woolly Farm!" she whispered to Benny and Violet. "I wouldn't be a bit surprised to find the Herr Bear here. Maybe she plans to copy him, too."

"Oh, hello, bears," Miss Sayer cried in her own chirpy voice. "Please come visit my cubs — and my Chatter Bear, of course. I'll take your picture with him."

The Three Bears posed in front of Chatter Bear. Their bear faces were smiling, but their real faces were frowning underneath.

"I've never seen your bears before," Jessie

SAYER'S
ALL NATURAL
CUBS

said in a deep voice she hoped Miss Sayer wouldn't recognize. "Are they new?"

Miss Sayer brought over one of the fleecy bears, whose stuffing wasn't quite tucked in. "Yes, they're my new line of bears — the old-fashioned kind that don't talk like my Chatter Bear here. Would you like to hold this one? It's stuffed with real fleece from real sheep."

Violet decided to learn more about Chatter Bear's new voice. "I heard your talking bear when he was in Doctor Firman's Toy Hospital. Didn't he say a different message a few days ago?"

Miss Sayer waved off Violet's question. "Oh, I'm just using him to get attention for my new bears. Everyone wanted to see a talking bear, but parents don't seem to want to buy one for their children," she said. "I've been told children like bears they can talk to, not the other way around. Is that true?"

Violet thought about Mister B. "Yes," she said, so quietly Miss Sayer didn't hear her. Not that it mattered, since she was already trying to interest another customer in her All-Natural Cubs.

With all the commotion going on with the Three Bears, Chatter Bear, and the new bears, Henry saw his chance. He squeezed himself into the booth. Bending down, he took a close look at some of Miss Sayer's new bears on the bottom shelf. He even searched behind some of them. Maybe he would find one bear that wasn't new — the one-of-a-kind Swiss Herr Bear. But Sayer's All-Natural Cubs were brand-new, all-of-a-kind bears.

"Well, don't you three bears want a few of my All-Natural Cubs to bring home?" Miss Sayer asked the Alden bears.

Benny couldn't stop himself from speaking up. "We like Peggy Bears!" he said, so loudly his voice rose even louder than Chatter Bear's.

Miss Sayer moved away. "Then I guess you're not interested in anything new and exciting." She turned to a child who had arrived with her mother. "Perhaps you are, young lady. Meet one of my new All-

Natural Cubs," Miss Sayer told the child. "Would you like to hold it?"

"The stuffing is coming out," the little girl said. "It's too skinny."

Miss Sayer bustled around the booth. "Not to worry. I've had so much . . . uh . . . interest in my bears, I had to order more before they were quite done. Let me show you what I can do."

Miss Sayer unlocked a small storage cabinet. She pulled out the orange tote bag that was never far from her. "See all this fleece?" She grabbed a fistful from her bag. "This is the finest lamb's wool around. That's what goes into my bears."

Henry overhead this. He stepped between Miss Sayer and the child. "Fleece like this goes into Peggy Bears, too. Where did you get it?"

For once, Miss Sayer couldn't speak. "From a farm," she finally answered, more slowly than usual.

"Oh, do you own a sheep farm?" the mother of the child asked. "With your own lambs?"

Miss Sayer took the rest of fleece from her bag. It began to expand into a big puff as she tried to come up with a truthful answer to the woman's question.

"No, actually, I don't have my own sheep farm."

"But I do."

The Three Bears, along with Henry and the other visitors, turned around.

Peggy Firman stood in Miss Sayer's booth, looking over the rows of copycat bears on the shelves.

Miss Sayer put her hand down on the fleece puff and tried to hide it. Of course, it was much too big to hide.

Jessie was too quick for Miss Sayer. "I need some stuffing, too," she said to the people in the booth. She patted her furry belly. "I didn't eat enough porridge."

Peggy broke into a smile. "Thank you, Papa Bear. My fleece somehow walked out of my barn without being on one of my sheep. I don't know how it happened, but I'm glad you helped me find it."

Miss Sayer went over to Chatter Bear.

She pushed a button. Finally the booth quieted down. "I'm sorry, Peggy. When Doc couldn't get Chatter Bear working, I decided he was right. Children want bears to cuddle, not to talk. So I decided to finish some bears I'd started last year and use some natural wool to stuff them. I didn't call them Hazel Bears, though."

"That's because you couldn't," Peggy said. "Putting your own name on these bears would have been wrong. You used some of my designs and now my wool fleece."

The customers began to drift away. Henry and the Three Bears stayed with Peggy.

"The day Peggy taught us how to sort fleece, were you up in the loft?" Henry asked.

Miss Sayer stared at Peggy. "Yes. You never let me help out with shearing the fleece or cleaning it. I wanted to learn how it was done in case my bear business became successful and I could buy a nice farm like Woolly Farm."

Peggy sighed. "Miss Sayer, Doc and I have offered you a great deal of help over the years. We even let you into the studio and the toy hospital to borrow things. But I couldn't give away *all* our secrets."

Miss Sayer held one of her bears so tightly some of the stuffing squeezed out. "I know, Peggy. I'm sorry. I get ideas, but then I don't stick with them very long. I like bears, but I can't figure out how to make children like *my* bears."

Peggy seemed a little less upset. "Well, that's the real secret, isn't it? Why don't you ask these three bears?"

Miss Sayer looked at the Aldens in their bear outfits. She still had no idea who they were. "Well, what's the secret about bears?"

Benny spoke up first. "They have to be fat, not skinny. And soft."

"They shouldn't talk too much," Violet said.

"Or be too big, because then you can't hold them," Jessie added.

"What about old bears?" Miss Sayer asked, forgetting everything the children had just told her. “I could find old bears, fix them up, and sell them for a lot of money. Yes, that’s an idea I never thought of.”

Henry looked at Miss Sayer. “Are you sure you never thought of it?”

CHAPTER 10

A Surprise Prize

The jamboree was so crowded, and the Aldens were so busy being bears, the last day arrived much too quickly.

"I finally finished sewing up Mister B. for the Best Bears Contest," Violet said when the children met outside the Town Hall.

Benny was worried about something. "How can we eat at the Teddy Bears' Picnic with our costumes on? The bear mouths are too small."

Henry laughed. "Not small enough for you to stop talking, Benny. I guess the three of you can take turns being people again."

"Peggy said it's okay to be half bears and half people at the picnic with our bear heads off," Jessie said. "She told me people like finding out who the Three Bears really are."

"I'd like to find out who our suspects really are," Jessie said. "I decided Miss Sayer isn't one of them."

The other children couldn't see Violet's thoughtful face under her costume. "I wish we could find out if Mrs. Keppel is really Elsa Berne. If she took Herr Bear, maybe she had a good reason."

Henry noticed Professor Tweedy walking quickly in the Aldens' direction. "What about him?" Henry asked. "We still don't know why he's been acting so strangely."

"For someone who reads bear books, he doesn't even seem to notice you're the Three Bears," Henry said when the professor passed by.

"I'm going to introduce myself," Jessie decided. "Maybe we'll get some clues from what he says." Jessie stepped in front of the professor. "Hello. I'm Papa Bear from *Goldilocks and the Three Bears.*"

This seemed to be a huge surprise to the professor. "Well, whoever put you in that costume should read a few different editions of the story. In the old books, the Three Bears do not grin like cartoon bears as you do in those costumes." The professor walked away, leaving the Aldens to wonder about him.

Violet lifted her arm to check her watch, but of course it was hidden beneath her costume. "Henry, isn't it almost time to show Mister B. to the judges? They're going into the hall. That's where Professor Tweedy went, too."

Henry checked his watch. "Time to go, with or without the Herr Bear. I guess all we can do now is keep an eye out for Mrs. Keppel and Professor Tweedy, too."

"Now Mister B. can keep two eyes out," Benny reminded everyone.

Streams of teddy bear lovers made their way into the Old Mills Town Hall. They brought their beloved bears in wagons, baskets, baby carriers, and strollers. There were bears of all shapes, sizes, and colors.

"Psst — there's Mrs. Keppel in front of the ladies' room," Jessie whispered to Violet. "She's got a baby carriage. Let's follow her. See you two later," she told Henry and Benny.

Mrs. Keppel gave Violet and Jessie a big smile when she saw them in their bear suits. "Ah, two of the Three Bears," she said to the girls, whom she didn't recognize. "Where is Baby Bear?"

Jessie nodded in Benny's direction. He was standing near the judges' table with Henry and Mister B. "He's over there."

Mrs. Keppel tried to push her carriage into the ladies' room when the security guard came by. "Sorry, no carriages in there, Mrs. Keppel. Don't worry, it's safe out here. I'll be just down the hall."

After the guard moved away, Jessie had an idea. "Would you like us to watch your carriage? After all, we're bear parents, too."

Mrs. Keppel laughed but hesitated. "*Ja* . . . I mean, yes. I shall be back within minutes."

Within seconds, Jessie tugged at the baby blanket covering the carriage.

"Two bears!" she and Violet cried at the same time when they saw two nearly identical bears staring back — one with blue eyes and one with golden eyes.

Violet quickly covered the bears again. "You were right, Jessie," she said. "Mrs. Keppel did take Herr Bear. I saw his eyes."

Mrs. Keppel returned. "*Danke*. I mean, thank you," she said. She pushed her carriage forward and walked off.

When the girls found Henry and Benny again, they had to wait to tell them their news. Grandfather was back and talking to Peggy, Doc, and Herr Bear's owner, Mrs. Withers. Even Miss Sayer was there, standing next to Mr. Alden. As always, she was holding Chatter Bear. Jessie's news would have to wait.

"Hi, Grandfather," Jessie whispered. "It's me under this costume, and Violet's in that costume." They took off the heads of their costumes so Grandfather could see their faces.

Grandfather hugged his plump, furry grand-bears. "You've been eating too many berries," he said, chuckling until he saw some long faces. "Oh, my, I'm afraid my joke won't cheer up this group. Doc already told me a valuable bear he was fixing for Mrs. Withers here was stolen from the toy hospital. Have you had any luck solving this mystery?"

"Follow me," Jessie said, waving everyone toward the front of the hall.

"Something's up," Violet whispered to the boys.

When the Aldens came to the judges' table, they were in for another surprise.

"Professor Tweedy!" Henry said. "What are you doing behind the judges' table?"

Unlike the smiling judges at the table, the professor looked as if he were about to examine machines, not sweet bears. "As you may know, I am a history professor," he explained. "I've been interested in historical bears since I wrote about President Theodore Roosevelt years ago."

Benny smacked his furry forehead. "I know why! My kindergarten teacher said teddy bears were named after him, because he wouldn't shoot a cub on a hunting trip. Neither would I."

The Aldens thought they saw a smile cross Professor Tweedy's face, but they couldn't be sure. "That's quite correct. Mr. Roosevelt was a very popular president, so some toy makers named their bears after him. Not that you'll see a genuine teddy bear here. They are extremely rare, as I wrote in one of my articles on bears."

Doc stepped forward to shake the professor's hand. "Why didn't you tell me you were an expert? I would have given you the run of my collection of bear magazines and books."

The professor looked over the top of his glasses at Doc. "Don't mention it. I helped myself to your library. Here," he said, opening his briefcase. "I borrowed these magazines. You can take them now. As for not telling anyone, I certainly didn't want all these people with their bears following and pestering me. I'm only here to judge the antique bears — those of historical interest."

That's when Jessie made her move. "What about these? Are they of historical interest?" She slowly pulled away the baby blanket covering Mrs. Keppel's bears.

"That's my bear!" Mrs. Withers cried. "That woman stole my bear."

Mrs. Keppel looked around at everyone. "I'm not ashamed at all that I took this bear. Look, Professor," she said, handing over two yellowed sheets of paper. "You will find my childhood name listing me as the parent of Fräulein Bear. My dear brother Kurt's name is on the Herr Bear birth certificate. The movers stole our bears when we had to leave our home in Switzerland. I have searched for my bear children for many years. Two years ago I found Fräulein. This week I found her twin, Herr Bear. I would have offered to buy him, but I don't have the money. I wasn't going to keep Herr Bear — I just wanted to have the two of them together for a short while. Herr Bear is all I have left to remind me of my dear brother."

Doc stepped forward. "I'm sad to say, Mrs. Keppel, that Mrs. Withers purchased the Herr Bear at an auction of rare toys years ago. I believe, after all this time, you cannot really claim Herr Bear as your own."

Mrs. Withers looked shocked. "I had no

idea that the bear was stolen," she said. "If I had known that there was someone who cared about it this much, I would have come looking for you a long time ago."

"What are you saying, Mrs. Withers?" asked Henry.

"I'm saying that this bear belongs with the person who loves it the most," said Mrs. Withers. "I have many more valuable bears in my collection. But it's clear to me that no bear would be more valuable to Mrs. Keppel than the Herr Bear. I'd like you to have it," she said, turning to Mrs. Keppel. "I only wish you had just told us all who you were to begin with."

Mrs. Keppel looked like she couldn't believe what she had just heard. Then she threw her arms around Mrs. Withers, crying tears of joy.

"Now, *that's* a bear hug," Benny said, grinning.

A few minutes later, the judges announced that it was time to judge the bears. They looked over table after table of bears and finally they made their decision.

Professor Tweedy put on his glasses, stood up, and tapped the microphone: "Ladies and gentlemen, I ask that you hold your applause until we name all the winners. For Friendliest Bear, we award the prize to the Aldens' Mister B."

Benny clapped by mistake, but luckily his bear paws didn't make any noise.

Professor Tweedy went on. "For Rarest Bear, the prize will be shared by Mrs. Henley Withers's Herr Bear and Mrs. Elsa Keppel's Fräulein Bear. Lastly, the judges have created a new prize for Most Talkative Bear. This prize goes to two bears: Chatter Bear, owned by Miss Hazel Sayer, and Baby Bear, not owned, but worn by Master Benjamin Alden."

Professor Tweedy couldn't keep people from clapping now. The winners came up to the table to have their pictures taken with their bears and their prizes — bear-shaped jars of honey.

For once, Benny got a word in before Chatter Bear: "I'm glad we solved the mystery. I couldn't bear it much longer."

GERTRUDE CHANDLER WARNER discovered when she was teaching that many readers who like an exciting story could find no books that were both easy and fun to read. She decided to try to meet this need, and her first book, *The Boxcar Children*, quickly proved she had succeeded.

Miss Warner drew on her own experiences to write the mystery. As a child she spent hours watching trains go by on the tracks opposite her family home. She often dreamed about what it would be like to set up housekeeping in a caboose or freight car — the situation the Alden children find themselves in.

When Miss Warner received requests for more adventures involving Henry, Jessie, Violet, and Benny Alden, she began additional stories. In each, she chose a special setting and introduced unusual or eccentric characters who liked the unpredictable.

While the mystery element is central to each of Miss Warner's books, she never thought of them as strictly juvenile mysteries. She liked to stress the Aldens' independence and resourcefulness and their solid New England devotion to using up and making do. The Aldens go about most of their adventures with as little adult supervision as possible — something else that delights young readers.

Miss Warner lived in Putnam, Connecticut, until her death in 1979. During her lifetime, she received hundreds of letters from girls and boys telling her how much they liked her books.